St Marys Institute

Congratulatory on the fiftieth anniversary of the ordination of his

Grace, Most Rev. J.M. Henni, D.D.

Archbishop of Milwaukee

St Marys Institute

Congratulatory on the fiftieth anniversary of the ordination of his Grace, Most Rev. J.M. Henni, D.D.
Archbishop of Milwaukee

ISBN/EAN: 9783741185311

Manufactured in Europe, USA, Canada, Australia, Japa

Cover: Foto ©Andreas Hilbeck / pixelio.de

Manufactured and distributed by brebook publishing software (www.brebook.com)

St Marys Institute

Congratulatory on the fiftieth anniversary of the ordination of his Grace, Most Rev. J.M. Henni, D.D.

CONGRATULATORY

ON THE

FIFTIETH ANNIVERSARY

OF

The Ordination

OF

HIS GRACE, MOST REV. J. M. HENNI, D.D.

ARCHBISHOP OF MILWAUKEE,

February 2d, 1879,

BY

The Young Lady Boarders

OF

ST. MARY'S INSTITUTE.

Chronostic Inscriptions

ON PYRAMIDS, INTERPRETED.

1829.

VIVat!

tIbI saCerDotI CVI Leo aLtarIs trIbVIt MysterIa.

Ein Bivat Dir, dem als Priester Leo (XII.) übergab des Altares Geheimnisse!

Long life to thee to whom, as Priest, Leo (XII.) entrusted the Altar's Mysteries.

1844.

a gregorIo tIbI JoannIs apostoLI

MVnVs DeCVs

epIsCopI onVs, nobIs LVX.

Von Gregor (XVI. kam) Dir des Apostels Johannes Amt und Würde, des Bischofs Bürde; und Licht.

From Gregory (XVI.) came to thee St. John the Apostle's office and dignity, the Bishop's burden; joy to us.

1875.

pII nonI faVore IVstItIaqVe

eCCe tIbI paLLII splenDoreM!

Durch Pius IX. Gunst und Gerechtigkeit: Sieh' da! für Dich des Palliums Glanz!

By favor and justice of Pius (IX.) behold for thee the Pallium's glory!

1879.

sVb aLtero Leone aVrea IVbILaeI Laetans Corona

reMane nobIs DVo LVstra!

Unter dem neuen Leo (XIII.) der goldenen Jubiläums-Krone Dich freuend, bleibe bei uns noch zwei Lustra (bis zum diamantenen Jubiläum).

Under the new Leo (XIII.) enjoy the golden jubilee's crown, and remain with us at least two more lustrums (to the diamond jubilee!)

CORONATION MARCH,   -   -   -   *Meyerbeer*

OPENING CHORUS.   -   -   -   *Prof. Singenberger*

> Salve Pater! gaudio plena, en!
> Filiarum Patri jubilanti
> Adjubilant corda.
> Tibi, nostræ domus ab initio
> Patri fideli!
> Excipe vota! Pater cœlestis
> Conservet Te nobis deprecantibus
> Sospitem, pium semper
> Patrem! Amen.

REMINISCENCES ITALIENNES,   -   -   *Oberthur*

CHORUS,   -   -   -   -   -   *Handel*

> Lo! he cometh, crowned with glory,
> Champion of the God of Might.
> Strew the victor fairest blossoms,
> Twine him garlands golden-bright.
> Fifty years he waged the warfare,
> Gained Jehovah's standard fame.
> Sound his praises, sing his triumph;
> Honor, glory to his name!

FIRST GARLAND — MYRTLE.

SOUVENIR OF THE HAPPY DAY OF ORDINATION.

Louder, louder swell the pæan, ring it out o'er land and sea,
By the clarion's sound proclaim it what this festive gathering be;
What is thrilling heart and spirit, mantling brow with joyous pride;
What has filled with exultation all Milwaukee's region wide.
No, 'tis not Milwaukee only, not this far Northwestern land,
For the sound of jubilation echoes, too, from distant strand;
Echoes loud 'mong Switzer Mountains, 'mong the Seven Hills of
    Rome,
'Mong the vine-clad hills and valleys where th' Ohio's waters foam;
Echoes in the crowded city, in secluded village dell,
In the wild wood where the Indian knows his God — his creed
    can tell.
Say it not, the world's forgetful, is not thinking of our theme;
Fancy not this joyous chorus is production of our dream;
For were voices not resounding of a hundred thousand strong,
Ah! the very stones would swell it and the glorious strain prolong.
Yes, one snowy slab of marble, on an altar far away,
Would uplift its voice and tell us of a joyous, joyous day
When the chosen one of Heaven, unto whom our tribute's due,
Sacrificed and sacrificing, near unto that alter drew.—
Let our spirits wander thither, mingle with that breathless throng,
And contemplate there the hero of our thrilling festal song.
Though he wears no wreath of laurel, wears no victor's garland fair,
Crowned with honor and with glory stands he noble, modest there.
Though no herald's trump proclaim them, valiant deeds that he
    hath done,
No triumphal arch give token of the victory he hath won,—
Hear ye not the angels chanting " Glory unto God most High"?
See them hovering, bending o'er him, as exultant he draws nigh!
Oh! those angel bands announce it unto all the courts above,

What this youthful, glorious champion hath achieved with arms
    of love :
How he severed bonds the strongest, sacrificed the near and dear;
Spent his youth in earnest labor to prepare for functions here,—
Functions such as know not hero fighting for his fatherland;
Exploits that no far-famed warrior e'er achieved with iron hand.
Oh! the fire in his bosom drove him o'er the stormy sea,
Here to fight Jehovah's battles, here to gain Him victory.
What his armor? where his weapons gleaming in his daring hand?
Lo! the priestly stole that vests him — sacred vessels at command.
Hark! those words of God-like power, at whose sound the demons
    flee,
And the hosts of Heaven hasten in his ranks enrolled to be!
Forth he goes to preach the Gospel, 'tis the sword he now must
    wield ;
Faith in Him that called him, sends him, is his safe and solid shield.
Has he fought unto this hour?   Has he trophies bright to show?
Greater, greater far, hereafter. he forthwith to win doth go.
Yes, his horn shall be exalted, glory crown his righteous name,
Blessings flowing on his pathway, after records shall proclaim.
What denotes that fair green garland, blossoms of the purest white?
And why throbs his heart so joyous?—All unearthly is his light!
Like the bridegroom from his chamber, goes he forth his course to
    run,
Steels with hope his youthful bosom, bears the Cross as standard on ;
Goeth to extend the kingdom of his glorious Spouse Divine —
Bring the Church his shining trophies, lay them down at her pure
    shrine.
'Tis his nuptial wreath all blooming; never, never shall it fade,
But shall grow still fairer, brighter, when with silver spray inlaid.
May we hope it? Shall we wait it?—count the years to twenty-five?
Will the hardship of that campaign his young spirit all survive?
Fear we not, for God hath found him as the prophet-king of old ;
His strong arm His own anointed shall with wisdom's might
    uphold.
Wait we but to see our hero show his valor to his King ;

Wait to hear his well-earned praises loud throughout the country
    ring.
Meanwhile to his angel's keeping is his myrtle wreath consigned,
Year by year new blossoms opening, lovelier still, to be entwined.

SERENADE,   -   -   -   -   *Schubert*

SECOND GARLAND—SILVER.

SOUVENIR OF THE TWENTY-FIFTH ANNIVERSARY.

Back again our spirits wander, back through *fifty* years agone,
To behold our youthful champion enter his career upon.—
Like the meek, beloved disciple, see him 'mong his flock appear,
With the bonds of Christ's affection drawing all unto him near.
Yes, he wields no other weapon than those arms of faith and love ;
And how rich the glorious conquest made for Him who reigns
    above !
Erring hearts cannot resist him — soon return to Jesus' arms ;
While, for luke-warm souls, Religion offers henceforth sweeter
    charms.
Young and old drink in the wisdom that his eager lips impart,
And the poor, the sick, the suffering find in him a father's heart.
How for ORPHANS he provideth, Cincinnati's people know,
Who, with grateful hearts, take pleasure there the stately walls to
    show
Of th' ASYLUM he erected, *first one in the West,* indeed,
Where forsaken Catholic children find a solace in their need.
For the CAUSE OF EDUCATION all unbounded is his zeal,
While his able pen he guideth for the country's proper weal.
Thus he labors, combats, struggles for Religion's cause alone,
Burning to promote God's glory, all forgetful of his own.—
Scarce have fifteen years thus vanished, shedding blossoms
    silver-bright,

When we see our young apostle in the Church a shining light;
For His humble servant's merits, God beholdeth not in vain,
Sees, to talents him entrusted, other five he still doth gain;
And from Rome His voice resoundeth, "Faithful thou hast been
    and true
Over few things that I placed thee; greater now shall be thy due.
I've received thy shining trophies, worthy offering for thy Spouse;
Enter into closer union, pay her now more solemn vows."—
Lo! it dawns, that blessed morning of St. Joseph's festive day,
And the priest before the altar stands that summons to obey,
Stands to swear his Lord allegiance while among his princes
    placed;
And his noble brow bends lowly, there to be with mitre graced.
Stands he shrinking from the contract he to-day shall enter in?
Shrinking from the fiercer combat which he knows must now begin?
Dreads he not the cross, still heavier, Heaven sends him thus to
    bear—
All the hardships, cares and trials falling henceforth to his share?
No; his helper, his protector, is the Lord; he knows not fear;
And, to all the Church demandeth, rings his "*Volo*" loud and
    clear.
Rings it but in that cathedral? in the sanctum of the Lord?
Have not angel-spirits caught it? Has not Satan's army heard?
Hark! above the glad Te Deum!—now that deep infernal groan!
For that "Volo" echoes, echoes far in Northwest regions lone.
Hear it, Red Men of the forest; hear those tidings of great joy!
Tremble, O dark pagan genius, for no more thy wiles decoy.
Yea, he comes, the Lord's anointed, huge Goliath to o'erthrow,
Comes to plant Jehovah's standard, to redeem from bondage low.
Is there not a tide prophetic rolling o'er the boundless main,
Wafting to Germania's borders—to the Alps, that joyful strain?
Swells it not with exultation 'mong the guardian spirits there?
Know they, for their happy charges, prospects open now so fair?
Ask the RECORDS OF WISCONSIN, what do her statistics show?
Why such tide of immigration see we to her back-woods flow?
Soon as comes her humble bishop, henceforth guiding star to be,

There 's attraction for the faithful e'en beyond the deep, blue sea.
He comes not as princely regent, in his purple vesture clad ;
Not a stately mansion opens unto him its portals glad ;
Not a bell peals out triumphant from a grand cathedral dome.
No ; *a lowly wooden building is his church — a cot his home.*
No procession comes to meet him, of a surpliced clergy-band —
One he sees, when morn approaches, offering at the altar stand.
'Tis his early friend, companion ; yes, with him he crossed the sea ;
Him kind Heaven has appointed his co-laborer to be !
Wide his field, a dreary region, dotted not with hamlets o'er,
Where the cross-surmounted steeple shows that faithful hearts
        adore ;
Yet are thousand Catholic settlers scattered in the woodlands drear ;
And no priest of God is with them, by the Gospel's light to cheer ;
None, to break the Bread of Heaven, souls that languish to sustain ;
None, to make for straying sinners with their Maker peace again ;
None, alas ! to give the Indian knowledge of his only good,
And to rank him with the faithful in a holy brotherhood.
Oh ! does not his courage falter while he scans this field of need ?
While he hears the very angels for his kind assistance plead ?
No ; his hope in God reposeth, who in him His work began ;
In His might He will perfect it, carry out His glorious plan !—
Let us, then, in spirit follow, the astounding scene to view,
Of a worthy prelate travelling in a manner strange and new ;
All alone, all unattended ; wanderimg through his realm so wide,
Braving dangers, countless hardships, for his sheep-fold to provide.
Oh! the Red Men of the forest can the thrilling story tell
Of the FIRST CHIEF BLACK-GOWN's VISIT to the wilds wherein they
        dwell ;
They can tell how oft they guided, carried him o'er dismal moor ;
How he hungered, patient suffered all the wants of Christ's own
        poor.
But oh! surely from those woodlands, from those marshes wild and
        drear,
There ascends a joyful anthem, our good Bishop's heart to cheer !
Hears he not the " Benedictus " swelling on the breeze of morn,

Praising God that to His people he hath raised salvation's horn ?
Grateful, hopeful throbs his bosom, yet escapes an anxious sigh ;
For how few are are still the laborers ready to this field to hie !
Greater yet must be his efforts all these yearning souls to save,
And he speeds o'er rolling ocean, there assistance meet to crave;
There, in hearts of zealous clergy, to enkindle more the fire
That consumes his own, and drives him e'er to aim still higher,
    higher.
How complacent God regardeth there his holy enterprise !
Giving him the blest assurance all his hopes to realize.
He returns ; but wherefore, think we?   Is it not to seek repose?
Not, indeed, our zealous Bishop, for a project new he knows.
To the Sunny South he hastens, down to Cuba, Mexico ;
There we see him humbly begging — see the Prelate stooping low !
Ah ! success must crown such efforts ; for he begs the funds to raise
To erect a FITTING TEMPLE FOR THE SACRIFICE OF PRAISE.
Yes, the happy day approaches when those hallowed walls shall
    ring
With the praises of Jehovah, while His priest is offering.
Hark ! from humble CONVENT CHAPEL, too, resounds that hymn of
    praise,
While a band of happy virgins hands and hearts to heaven raise ;
For our Blessed Lady's daughters have the Prelate's call obeyed,
To INSTRUCT THE LITTLE CHILDREN — lend their guardian
    angels aid.
And the ORPHANS are provided, lisping glad their Father's name;
While THE SICK, IN THEIR ASYLUM, his paternal love may claim.—
Thus the years are speeding onward, bringing blessings more and
    more,
In the Bishop's cornucopia day by day anew to pour ;
While the light of Faith, like magic, through the dismal forest
    streams,
And, anon, the Cross triumphant, reared on village turret, gleams.
Oh ! how cheering is that shimmer ! like the softest silver light
Shed upon earth's weary exiles by the gentle queen of night.

Streams it not in grateful bosoms ?   Beams it not in heav'n-turned
     eye ?
Surely, there are tens of thousands wafting thanks beyond the sky !
Now 'tis gone — the last bright annum ; for our date is '54 ;
Since our panorama opened, twenty-five we 've counted o'er!
Yes, completed is the garland of those SILVER-BLOSSOMS fair,
And behold! a glorious chaplet for that noble brow to wear !
Lo! " With honor thou hast crowned him," now the Church
     exultant sings,   .
And "His horn thou hast exalted in the sight of earthly kings."

FANTASIE—SEMIRAMIDE,   -   -   -   -   *Rossini*

THIRD GARLAND—GOLDEN JUBILEE.

Once again a panorama fair and charming let us view,
While the passing years we number up to twenty-five anew.
More intense the light is growing, like the golden morning's smile,
When the gentle moon, too feeble, fadeth from our view the while.
Into frowning, grand old forests, see it streaming more and more ;
For the woodman's axe is ringing near his humble cabin door,
And those giant trees majestic, by its stroke are lowly felled,
While the white men homes are rearing where the Indian council held.
Where once stood his smoking wigwam, where loud rang his battle
     cry,
There the pioneer's grand anthem swells triumphant to the sky.
And how oft the bell is swinging in new churches just complete ;
For their Bishop glad to welcome, see the parish children meet.
Oh! how throbs his heart exultant, Jesus' chosen one to be,
Thus to bless His habitation, and His smile of grace to see.
Ever fresh on memory's tablet shall that blessed year remain,
When he TWENTY-FIVE such conquests for his glorious Spouse doth
     gain.

All the more his joy is heightened when to CHURCH is nestling near,
Too, a pleasant SCHOOL-HOUSE ready for the little ones so dear.
Now his heart no more is bleeding that no shepherds he can send,
All these flocks of growing lambkins with a zealous care to tend;
For, behold! it is erected — in its stately beauty reared,—
The SALESIANUM building, in our annals so revered.
Yes; the plan by God inspired when he knelt at foreign shrine,
Glorious do those walls reveal it, bathed in Heaven's bright sunshine;
And the saint upon whose relics then his lips he fervent pressed,
Smiles upon this work prodigious, through his intercession blest.
Ah! we see that signal blessing in a lofty mind displayed,
Of whose zealous, mighty efforts God himself the choice had made.
Who can give the joy expression, thrilling deep the Bishop's heart,
When this champion stood before him, plans he nurtured to impart.
Here he knew was God's own finger to promote the enterprise,
And his soul sent forth thanksgiving to the throne of the All-wise.
In that strain joined bands of angels, joined apostles' glorious choir;
Knew they not God's day of favor for the West drew nigher, nigher?
See those college portals open unto youths from far and near;
From them, see the priest doth issue, to begin his great career!
Yes; how many of God's servants, laboring as apostles true,
Grateful bless their Alma Mater, ne'er forgetting what is due
To our zealous Bishop's project of a holy work so grand,
And the gifted men that offered him their eager, helping hand.
Thus we see, like golden blossoms, joys spring up each year anew,
And the field to him entrusted groweth brighter to our view.
Seeds he sowed, in tears, are yielding GOLDEN HARVEST richer still;
Lo! with it the joyous angels now his cornucopia fill.
And his flock, how doth it prosper with these blessings manifold,
While resources for its welfare wider, grander we behold!
INSTITUTIONS NEW ARE THRIVING, JESUS' NAME TO GLORIFY,
And the worldly-wise beholdeth purer founts the Church supply.
Ah! the Bishop, with emotion, as his realm he now surveys,
Calls to mind how scenes have altered since those early, gloomy days.
With his staff he crossed its borders, like the patriarch of yore,
And behold! how God hath blessed him with this smiling, bounteous
    store!

Hath He made him, then, the promise thus his fold to multiply
Like the sands upon the seashore, like the stars in azure sky?
Yes; so great is now his people that the Church is filled with joy
To relieve his care of ruling, and new bishops to employ.
Thus the wilderness hath budded, and the desert is made glad,
In its beauty like to Sharon and to Carmel it is clad;
For the glory of Mount Libanus is given it that day
When three princes of God's kingdom over it His sceptre sway.
But the height of its full splendor we behold it then attain
When our Bishop's shining merits him the PALLIUM do gain;
When the great Eternal City sends her envoys to our shore,
And Milwaukee scenes doth witness as the West ne'er saw before.
Then, indeed, with robe of glory doth the Church her spouse adorn;
Then doth God fulfil His promise to exalt His servant's horn.
Yea, has not our Saviour said it, He himself will glorify
Whosoe'er to give Him glory doth his life on earth apply?
Lo! it streameth down already, what awaits beyond the skies,
When Milwaukee's FIRST GOOD BISHOP is ARCHBISHOP made, likewise!
Thus kind Heaven hath decreed it, ere approach the FIFTIETH year
Since we saw our young apostle first set out on his career.
Hail! all hail! that day of glory draweth for our Prelate nigh!
See! Aurora's portals open in the ruddy eastern sky,
Open on the fiftieth morning since he welcomed glad the day
When he was the first time vested in his priestly full array.
Though the breath of morn is frosty, though all Nature's lone and
        drear,
There is beauty, joy and glory in Milwaukee's happy sphere;
For what scene can yet be fairer, celebration more sublime
Than this DAY OF JUBILATION ushers in with solemn chime?
Hark! cathedral bells are pealing — List! that hymn of lofty cheer!
Oh! how joyous does it echo in the convent chapel near!
Sacrificing at the altar, our exultant Pontiff see,
While above the angels hover with his WREATH OF JUBILEE!
Drooping from his cornucopia, how it teems with blossoms bright,
With those FIFTY YEARS of merit, bathed in Heaven's golden light.
God alone the value knoweth of each leaflet in that spray,

And the glory it bespeaketh on the great accounting day,
With a thrill of joy we view it, as the emblem, meet and fair,
Of the crown our sainted Prelate shall, enthroned, in Heaven wear.

CHORUS.

> Great and marvelous are thy works,
>   Lord, God Almighty!
> Just and true are thy ways,
>   Thou King of Saints.
> Who shall not praise thee?
>   Who shall not glorify thy name?

Trio in the distance, during which
TABLEAU.

Monumental Cross, ends ornamented with the sacerdotal, episcopal and
archiepiscopal insignia.

Inscription: — Qui legitime certat, coronatur.
Above, the unfinished crown, held by angels.

———— ❖ ————

EPILOGUE.

Fancy joyed the scene to picture, when the hero of our song
Entered first upon the warfare he hath glorious waged so long.—
With a thrill of exultation let us now the sequel view,
While we pay our grateful tribute — honor to whom honor's due.
Here a monument's erected, such as ne'er the conqueror saw
Of a hostile army fettered, groveling 'neath his iron law.
No; this is the glorious trophy of a champion far more famed,
Who, beneath Religion's standard, has more brilliant vict'ries gained!
On it we behold engraven tokens of his conquests made,
While the garlands that have crowned him, breath of Time shall
    never fade.
LAWFUL HATH CHRIST'S HERO STRIVEN — GLORIED IN THE CROSS
    ALONE,—

AND THE CROWN OF JUSTICE WAITS HIM; waits him the apostle's throne.
Angel spirits hold that dower for the one we so revere,
Still to add more precious jewels, as we trust, for many a year.

Thus permit us, honored Prelate, on thy glorious jubilee,
To express the wish that's foremost in each heart that throbs for thee.
Long be yet thy stay among us, long and glorious thy career!
While the scene we here have pictured day by day thy spirit cheer.
Oh! we 're filled with joy, great Prelate, in reviewing years now past,
That so radiant is the halo even now around thee cast.
And, while yet our fancy lingers, all enraptured with the sight,
Hark! a sweet refrain is wafted, filling us with new delight.
How it echoes and re-echoes, like the tone of silvery bells,
As from heart's o'erflowing fountain, with a thrilling gush, it wells.
'T is Milwaukee's grateful anthem for the glory on her shed;
For the blessings, worthy Prelate, thou hast labored so to spread;
For the Cross thou hast so willing for her children's welfare borne—
All the hardships for them suffered, and the trials undergone;
For the precious seeds of wisdom thou hast sown into their hearts;
For the patronage extended unto science and the arts.—
Full of joy, Saint Mary's pupils eager hearts and voices blend
In this sweet harmonious chorus, warm and cordial thanks to tend
For the true, paternal kindness shown to inmates of these walls;
For the many special favors memory on this day recalls.
In the annals of the Convent they are all recorded fair —
Deeper still in hearts engraven, that forget them not in pray'r.
Oh! could we, Most Reverend Father, add one shining little ray
To the light that shimmers glorious from thy GOLDEN WREATH to-day!
Could we in thy cornucopia gratitude's best tokens pour,
Surely, with the richest treasures thou wouldst see it flowing o'er!
But we need the wish not utter; speaks not heart unto the heart?
Yes; a Heart Divine hath heard it — heard benignly to impart
What alone can recompense thee for the lasting debt we owe;
What thy joy complete can render even in this vale of woe.
Vale of tears — how can we mention word so sad in this glad hour?
Yet, this scene, itself so joyful, speaks it with a startling power.

Lo! thy crown, Most Reverend Father, tho' it beams transcendent
    fair,

Angels hold it — not yet finished — for thine honored brow to wear.
Many a priceless, brilliant jewel must beset it, grace it still;
Crimson crosses glow upon it — thus the blessed word fulfill:
"When he hath been tried and proven, in the furnace tried like gold,
Then the crown of life prepared him shall his sainted eye behold."
Oh! rejoice then, worthy Prelate, looking forward to that day,
Make thy crown the more resplendent; long, oh long! still with us
    stay.

Carry it still longer, Father, that sweet Cross, thy portion blest,
Of the one that opened for us portals of eternal rest.
Oh! when once those gates are lifted on thy coronation morn,
May still many years of merit then that chaplet rich adorn.
Like to peerless gems the FIFTY that have passed beset it now,
But be brightest ones still added ere it grace thy sainted brow!

TRIO.—

    Hark! what mean those holy voices
      Sounding sweetly through the sky?
    Are not angel-forms descending,
      Drawing softly to us nigh?
    See! they hold a crown of glory,
      While they hover full of joy,
    Singing, " Glory to the Highest!
      " Glory be to God on high!"

    Lo! that fair and radiant chaplet,
      Graced with many a precious gem,
    Is our worthy Prelate's dower,
      Is his glorious diadem!
    Fifty years of saintly merit
      Now that brilliant crown beset, ·
    While the fairest, richest, brightest,
      Angel-hands are adding yet.

Joyous are those spirits waiting
  For the coronation day,
When, in glory to enthrone him,
  They shall bear his soul away.
Sing we, with the hosts celestial,
  Glory be to God on high,
Who hath blest His own anointed,
  Thus His name to glorify.

CHORUS.

Hallelujah ! hallelujah !
Salvation and honor and glory and power
Unto the Lord our God!
All ye his servants praise our God ;
All ye that fear Him, both small and great.
Hallelujah ! hallelujah !
Salvation and honor and glory and power !
For the Lord God omnipotent reigneth.
Hallelujah! hallelujah !

ROSA MYSTICA.

Perſonen:

Engel der Vorſehung.   Fünf Erbenſöhne.

Comp. by Rev. Katzer.

Rosa Mystica.

Prolog.

O Jubelfest, dem gilt die heut'ge Feier,
Du lockst in graue Vorzeit uns zurück!
Ja, lüften wir der alten Jahre Schleier,
Zu schau'n im Geiste Edens golden Glück!
Dort auf des Paradieses wonn'gen Fluren
Einst wandelt froh das erste Menschenpaar;
Anbetend staunt es ob der Allmacht Spuren,
Und bringt mit Dank sein erstes Opfer dar.
Horch! es erschallen rings die reinen Lüfte
Von sel'ger Geister hehrem Jubelchor;
Und sieh! es steigen süße Rosendüfte
Auf lichten Zephyrschwingen hoch empor.
Zu jenen gold'nen Zeiten hauchten Rosen
Des Himmels süßen, reinsten Wohlgeruch;
Des Paradieses Au'n die sündenlosen,
Sie kannten nicht Jehova's Zornes Fluch.
Doch ach, — es kam die unheilvolle Stunde,
In der die erste Sünde ward verübt;
Und donnernd scholl der Fluch aus Gottes Munde,
Der Edens golden Glück für immer trübt.
Hinaus in öde, unbebaute Räume
Der Herr das sünd'ge Menschenpaar verwies;

Rosa Mystica.

Prolog.

O Jubelfest, dem gilt die heut'ge Feier,
Du lockst in graue Vorzeit uns zurück!
Ja, lüften wir der alten Jahre Schleier,
Zu schau'n im Geiste Edens golden Glück!
Dort auf des Paradieses wonn'gen Fluren
Einst wandelt froh das erste Menschenpaar:
Anbetend staunt es ob der Allmacht Spuren,
Und bringt mit Dank sein erstes Opfer dar.
Horch! es erschallen rings die reinen Lüfte
Von sel'ger Geister hehrem Jubelchor:
Und sieh! es steigen süße Rosendüfte
Auf lichten Zephyrschwingen hoch empor.
Zu jenen gold'nen Zeiten hauchten hier
Des Himmels süßen, reinsten Seligkeit
Des Paradieses Au'n die frommen
Sie kannten nicht Jehova's
Doch ach, — es kam die
er die erste Sünde

Nur fieberhafte, trügerische Träume
Ihm malten tückisch vor das Paradies.
Nur in des Schlafes falschen Lichtgeweben
Umweht den Menschen süßer Rosen Hauch;
Er greifet freudig sie zu brechen eben,
Wacht auf, — sich ritzend an dem Dornenstrauch.
Umsonst des Paradieses Freudenrose
Sucht das verbannte, arme Menschenherz;
Und von der Erde unfruchtbarem Schooße
Blickt es vertrauend, sehnend himmelwärts.
Wie sich der Zukunft graue Wolken lichten,
Als ob des Tages gold'ner Anbruch nah! —
Und aus der fernen, fernen Jahre Schichten
Ihm glänzt entgegen Rosa Mystica.
Ist Edens Glück auf ewig nicht entzogen? —
So frägt es hoffend, lebt wieder neu.
Wohl Satans List hat schändlich mich betrogen,
Daß besser ich erkenne Gottes Treu. —
Mit frischem Muth bebaut der Mensch die Erde.
Rinnt von der Stirne auch der saure Schweiß,
Versüßet ihm ja jegliche Beschwerde
Der goldnen Rosa Mystica Verheiß.
Gern segnet Gott des Menschen büßend Mühen
Nach liebevoller, väterlicher Weis';
Läßt ihm am Dornstrauch manche Ros' erblühen,
An die geheimnißvolle mahnend leis.
Des Schicksals Engel beut nach Gottes Willen
Den Adamskindern diese Rosen dar;
Des Herzens Sehnen sie wohl nimmer stillen;
Denn nimmer stillt es, was die Zeit gebar.

Engel der Vorsehung am Rosenhügel.

Kaum hat der erste Strahl des jungen Tages
Begrüßt die grünen, thaubeperlten Auen,
Kaum die Natur dem Schlafe sich entwunden,
Erwacht auf's Neu im Menschenherz das Sehnen
Nach dem verscherzten Paradieses=Glück,
Das jeder sich nach seinem Sinne malt.
Ich höre leises Flüstern, höre Tritte :
Wohl wieder eine Gruppe Adamskinder.—
Was habt in diesen Räumen ihr verloren?

Erdensöhne.

Verloren? ach nicht wir ; nein, unser Vater
Verlor uns Edens holde Freudenrosen,
Die da Jahrtausend' schon die Nachwelt sucht.
Der Schöpfer hat sie Deiner Hand vertraut :
Du guter Engel, laß Dich rühren, bitte,
Nach Wunsch brich Jedem eine Rose ab !

1. Erdensohn.

Gib mir des Reichthums glanz= und blätterreiche !
Dann bin ich glücklich, wird mir nichts gebrechen;
Genieße dann nach voller Herzenslust
Die Freuden, so die Welt in Fülle beut.

Engel.

Es sei ! Nimm hin das Pfand des Glücks ! Doch wisse,
Die Sorgen, die der Reichthum mit sich führt,
Sind Dornen, die oft tief das Herz verwunden.

2. Erdensohn.

Nie kann Genuß noch Reichthum mich beglücken,
Ohn' Freund, der theilt mit mir des Lebens Freuden ;
Allein genöß' ich sie zur Hälfte nur.
O theile mir der Freundschaft Rose zu !

Engel.

Die Freundschaft ist ein schätzenswerthes Gut!
Es sei Dir nicht versagt! Doch wo der Freund,
Deß Treu in Trübsal sich bewährt hienieden?
Die Liebe wo, die keine Trennung kennet?

3. Erbensohn.

Des Reichthums Ros' ich nicht verschmäh', noch auch
Der wahren Freundschaft Glück; doch bitte, schenk'
Aus Deiner Rosenfüll' die dritte mir!
Bewahre mir der Jugend Rosen, so
Des Lebens Frühling auf die Wangen malet!
Laß nicht des Alters Schnee mein Haupt bedecken!
Des Todes kalte Hand wend' gnädig ab!

Engel.

Du thöricht Erdenkind, — Dein Wunsch kann nimmer
Erfüllet werden : ein Gesetz hat Er
Gegeben ; nimmer wird Er's überschreiten,
Es ist das schreckliche Gesetz des Todes.

4. Erbensohn.

Des Goldes falscher Glanz mein Aug' nicht blendet,
Noch möchte im Vergnügens=Taumel ich
Des Lebens Kräfte nutzlos schwinden lassen ;
Gern steig hinab ich in die kühle Gruft,
So mir das selige Bewußtsein bleibt,
Daß auf dem Rasenhügel mir erblühe
Des Ruhmes Ros' als Dichter oder Held !

Engel.

Wie Dunst und Rauch verfleucht die eitle Ehre,
Zwar soll die Rose, die Du suchst, Dir werden :
Bald aber wird entblättern sie der Sturm
Der göttlichen Gerechtigkeit, weil Du
Geraubt dem Schöpfer, was nur ihm gebührt,

Die Ehre. — Noch ein Adamsfohn sich naht
Behenden Schrittes. Sag' mir Deine Wahl!

5. Erbenfohn.

Die Wahl, o guter Engel, steht bei Dir.
Den Engel der Vorsehung sieht in Dir
Mein gläubig Aug', verehrt mein gläubig Herz.

Engel.

Da gläubig Du die Wahl mir überlassest,
Hör', was ich Dir in Gottes Namen künde:
Die Rosen, die den Erdenkindern blühen,
Sie werden nie Dein edel Sehnen stillen;
Drum brech' von diesen Rosen ich Dir keine.
Drei Himmelsrosen sind beschieden Dir.

"Beatus homo qui invenit sapientiam et
qui affluit prudentia: Melior est acquisitio
ejus negotiatione argenti, et AURI primi et
purissimi fructus ejus. Prov. III. 13. 14.

„Glückselig der Mensch, der die Weisheit
findet und Klugheit in Fülle hat. Ihr
Gewinn ist besser als der Handel mit
Silber, und ihre Früchte sind besser als
das beste, feinste Gold." Spr. III. 18. 14.

Des Höchsten heil'ger Wille ist, daß Dir
Im schönsten Garten seiner ewigen Stadt
Der wahren Weisheit Rose sich entfalte,
Im Moose der Bescheidenheit verhüllet.—
Der Freudenthräne Glanz verräth des Herzens
Verborg'nen Wunsch. — Eh' sie dem Aug' entperlet,
Mag sie zur Wehmuthsthräne sich gestalten.

"In igne probatur AURUM et argentum,
homines vero receptibiles in camino
humiliationis. Ecclus. II. 5.

„Silber und G o l d wird durch's Feuer geprüft ;
die Lieblinge Gottes aber im Ofen der Demüthi=
gung." Sir. 2. 5.

Es wartet Dein die rothe Leidensrose.

Das wilde Dorngestrüpp der neuen Welt,
Columbia's golb= und elenbreicher Boden
Ist Dir zum Arbeitsfelde angewiesen,
Dem Herrn zu winnen, wie die Jünger einst,
Der Seelen viel und schön ohn' alles Maaß.

5. E r b e n s o h n.

Und ganz allein soll ich den Sturmeswogen
Des weiten Ozeans mich anvertrauen ?
Allein die unbekannten Pfade wandeln.
Die Füße ritzend an den Dornen wund ?

E n g e l.

Nicht doch mein Sohn ; dafür hat Gott gesorgt. —
"Amico fideli nulla est comparatio
et non est digna ponderatio AURI et
argenti contra bonitatem fidei illius." Ecclus VI. 15.

„Mit einem treuen Freunde ist nichts zu
vergleichen ; und der Werth seiner Treue
wiegt G o l d und Silber auf." Sir. 6. 15·

Ein solcher Freund ist Dir vom Herrn bescheert,
Er theil' die Leiden Dein, sowie die Freuden,
Sei Stütze Dir und Trost in's Greisen=Alter.

"Astitit regina a dexteris tuis in vestitu
DEAURATO." Ps. XLIV. 10.

„Die Königin steht zu Deiner Rechten im
g o l d e n e n Kleide." Ps. 44.— 10.

Im framben Land' hat Dir zur Braut erkoren
Der Herr die Kirche sein im Goldgewand,
Der Du nach Heilands Vorbild sollest werden
Ein Blut= und Schmerzensbräutigam.

5. Erbensohn.

Wie lieblich
Ertönt das Wort von jener hehren Braut,
Die meine erste, einz'ge Liebe sei!
Vor Blut und Schmerzen aber graut dem Herzen,
Das ja zur Freud' ursprünglich ist geschaffen.

Engel.

Zur Freude wohl, doch erst durch Leib erreicht,
Es seiner Schöpfung hohes Ziel.

5. Erbensohn.

Und wenn
Vom Dorn der Leidensros' zerstochen ist
Das arme Herz; gibts keinen Balsam dann,
Der Heilung in die Wunde kühlend träufle?

Engel..

Mir schien, als ob erfaßtest Du das Wort
Von jener Braut im Goldgewand. Nun sieh'
Am Trau-Altar sie reicht als heilig Pfand
Der Treue unverletzt der Rosen dritte,
Die Rosa Mystica der Priesterweihe,
Vom Gnadenborn auf Golgatha begossen.
Will fürder nicht die Zukunft Dir enthüllen,
Bleib' treu der angewies'nen Bahn. Lebwohl!
Auf Wiedersehn!
Ja, wiedersehen werd'
Ich Dich, Du auserlesen Adamskind!
Eh' Deines Lebens Sonne golden sinket
Wird eine selt'ne Rose Gott Dir weihen,
Weil irdische hochherzig Du verschmäht.

Abſchiedslied . . . . **Prof. Singenberger.**

Nimmer darf des Geiſtes Weh'n
Der Erwählte wiederſtehn.
Als den Ruf vom Weſten fern
Er vernahm, da folgt er gern.
Mit dem Freunde Hand in Hand
Zieht er in das ferne Land.
Weit weg von dem jungen Rhein
Vom berühmten Gnadenſchrein,
Wo vom Früh= und Spätroth glänzt
Rings die Alpe eisbekränzt :
Mutter Heimath, nun abe,
Ob das Scheiden thue weh!
Wo die Rothhaut kriegt und jagt,
Wo der Urwald rieſig ragt,
Da auf weiten Wüſtenei'n
Harren reiche Ernten mein ;
Mutter, in Maria's Hut
Laß ich Dich ; ſie hütet gut.

Barkerole.   Die Winde wehen, das Ruder knarrt
Die Segel blähen ſich ſchon zur Fahrt
O wache mir Madonne, der Gnadenmilde voll
O Land der ſtillen Wonne, o Heimat fahre wohl !
O Heimat fahre wohl !

SELECTIONS—Gounod's Opera,   -   *Ketterer and Durand*

TABLEAU VIVANT.

Wirkungskreis.

Frohlocke, jauchze Himmel Du und Erde !
Gekommen iſt die Fülle nun der Zeit,
Aus Gottes Mund erſchallt ein neues Werde,

Ertönt ein Fiat der Barmherzigkeit.
Der Wurzel Jeffe ist ein Zweig entsproffen,
Und Rosa Mystica, geschaut von Fern
Dereinst, die Blume hold, die sich erschloffen,
Die Blume, auf der ruht der Geist des Herrn.
Es kam der Tag, der aller Welt Verlangen,
Den Abraham im Geist frohlockend sieht,
Das Heil, dem Simeon und Anna sangen
Ihr nie verhallend hehres Kirchenlied, —
Als in dem Opferkelch der Ros' geweihet
Zur Sühne ward die Perle unschätzbar,
Als Die vom Herrn so hoch gebenedeiet,
Im Tempel bracht den Erstgebor'nen dar.
„Laß Herr im Frieden Deinen Diener scheiden,
Da meine Augen hier noch sah'n Dein Heil,
Die Ehre Israels, das Licht der Heiden,
Der Welt Verlangen, der Gerechten Theil!"
So tönt es aus des greisen Sehers Munde
Beim ersten, würd'gen Offertorium ;
O der erhab'nen sel'gen Weihestunde
Des neuen Bunds im alten Heiligthum!
O Rosa Mystica, gebenedeite,
Du Priesterin an Gottes Hochaltar!
Dein heilig Recht übt aus der Neugeweihte,
Der zitternd bringt sein erstes Opfer dar.
O Rosa Mystica der Priesterweihe,
Die über Engel selbst den Staub erhebt!
Was ist der Mensch, daß ihm der Herr verleihe
Gewalt, vor der ja selbst der Seraph bebt?—
O Kirche Gottes! Braut im Sternenkranze!
Dem Jüngling Wohl! der sich mit Dir vermählt.
Du strahlest ewiglich im Jugendglanze,
Wer Dich erkor, hat wahrlich gut gewählt.
Dir Priester Heil! am bräutlichen Altare,

Die Königin zu Deiner Rechten stand ;
Seither verflossen fünfzig Lebensjahre,
Und nun erblickst Du sie im Goldgewand.

DUETT – PIANOS,   -   -   -   -   *C. M. von Weber.*

Engel.

Die Rosen, die vor mehr als fünfzig Jahren
Dem Jünglinge von Gott verheißen worden,
Sie schmücken nun den silberhaar'nen Greis.
Gar herrlich hat mit ihren fünfzig Blättern
Die Rose seines priesterlichen Amtes
Entfaltet sich, benetzt von Leidenszähren.
Wie jedes Blatt, im Thau der Gnade schimmernd,
Den Duft der Tugend, des Verdienstes haucht !
Was ehedem nach ew'ger Weisheit Absicht
Verborgen ihm—der Zeiten Wellen spülten
Es an das Licht. Mit jedem Jahr sich mehrt
Der Rose Glanz, verbreitet weiter sich
Ihr süßer Wohlgeruch nach Nord und West
Und Süd und Ost—zur Siebenhügel-Stadt ;
Den Stellvertreter Christi selbst erfreuend.
Wie er die Rosa Mystica, die still
Im Thal geblüht, erhebt, der Ceder gleich
Des Libanon ! Der Rose neue Zierde,
Dem Priester neue Würde Papst Gregor
Verleiht ; die Mitra und der Hirtenstab
Der Rose fünfzehn' Blatt gar herrlich schmücken !
O duftend Blatt der seligsten Erinn'rung
Für Tausend, aber Tausend, die in Dir,
Hochwürdigster, voll fünf und dreißig Jahr
Den treuen Bischof ihrer Seelen ehren.
Excelsior ! In lichtern Höhen noch
Soll glänzen Deine Rosa Mystica !

Sieh da des Rosenmonats dritter Tag,
Des Jahres Achtzehnhundert fünf und siebzig
In Zügen unvertilgbar eingravirt!
Der Tag, da Pius Neunter unvergeßlich—
Dir übersendete das Pallium,
Das Dich erhob zum mächt'gen Kirchenfürsten.
Noch fallen in des Volkes Herzen wieder
Des schönen Tages volle Freudenklänge,
An dem wir Dich als Erzbischof begrüßt.
Ihr fünfzig Blätter dieser Wunderrose,
Die manches Herz mit ihrem Duft erquickt!
O, daß ihr fünfzig Blätter Zungen hättet!
Verkünden solltet ihr den Ruhm des Mannes,
Den Gott geprüft wie Gold und seiner werth
Gefunden. Künden auch den Ruhm des Freundes,
Der treulich ihm bis jetzt zur Seite stand,
Der mit ihm theilt des heut'gen Tages Feier.
Wozu in Worte kleiden, was die Welt
Mit Augen sieht? Die Priesterschaar mag reden,
Das dankerfüllte Volk, die Gotteshäuser,
Die Lehr-Anstalten und die Klostermauern,
Sie mögen Zeugniß geben diesen Männern,
Und deren Wirken. Ehr' wem Ehr' gebührt!
So hieß es bei den Griechen schon und Römern.
Sieh'! wie sie um den Lorbeer eifrig ringen
Und um die Siegespalme muthig kämpfen!
Sieh' wie der Kranz von Eichenlaub die Stirn
Des Edlen schmücket! Auch die Nachwelt wußte
Nicht minder das Verdienst zu schätzen. Zähle,
Wer kann, die Ordensstern' und Ehrentitel,
Die Fürsten-Dankbarkeit dem Held verleiht!
Doch unter diesen Ehrenzeichen Einem
Der Vorzug wohl gebührt: der gold'nen Rose,
Geweiht vom heil'gen Vater und gewidmet
Den Fürsten, die durch Treue sich im Kampf

Für Gottes und der Kirche Recht bewährt.
Gegönnet sei'n den Fürsten ihre Rosen,
Die goldenen. Dein Aug', Hochwürdigster,
Sich nicht an Goldes Glanz ergötzt ; dein Streben
Gleich Sanct Johannes kühnem Adlerflug
Weit höher zielet, nach der Gottheit Schooß ;
Sie war Dein Theil von Jugend auf ; drum soll,
Nachdem des Lebens Silberschnur zerreißet
Und sich die gold'ne Binde löst,—Dein Lohn,
Dein ewiger, die Perle sein, die sich
Im Kelch der Rosa Mystica geopfert.
Die Gottheit, die Du mit geweihten Händen
Zu tausend Mal der Gottheit dargebracht ;
Die goldne Ros', die mystische, nimm hin,
Hochwürdigster, zur gold'nen Jubelfeier,
Die gold'ne Ros' mit ihren fünfzig Blättern,
Von Gottes Vorsehung Dir zuerkannt,
Und Dir im Himmelsgarten aufbewahrt.
Den Wunsch zugleich nimm hin, Hochwürdigster,
Daß, uns zum Trost, zur Freud, noch manches Blatt
Der Rose Dein sich reihe an.

"Ut probatio vestrae fidei multo pretiosor
AURO (quod per ignem probatur)
inveniatur in laudem et gloriam et
honorem in revelatione Jesu Christi". I. Petr. I. 7·

„Damit die Prüfung Eures Glaubens
viel köstlicher als durch Feuer erprobtes
G o l d erfunden werde zum Lobe und Preise
und zur Ehre bei der Erscheinung Jesu Christi."
I. Petr. I. 7.

CHORUS, - · · · · · *Prof. Singenberger*

Quot Deum affectibus
Cor tuum magnificat
Qui te tot effectibus
Gratiae laetificat.

Dicis :   Deo Gratias !
Dicis :   Laudo Te Deum !
Calice qui satias
Tam praeclaro cor meum.

Cui tu a puero jam
Obedisti genio
Per virtutis semitam
Hoc te ornat senio.

Defuere non tibi
Poenae rosae rubeae
Albae neque gaudii
Florent nunc et aureae.

Quae in calice tuo
Decem lustra pistica
Arsit rosa, denuo
Beet Rosa Mystica !

CONGRATULATIONS

OF

ST. MARY'S CONVENT DAY PUPILS.

To the temple of Sion, in splendor profuse,
　　Far surpassing in richness the Orient's climes,
In the robes of sweet virginal beauty arrayed,
　　Comes pure Mary, the " Lily of Israel's " times.

In her arms gently bearing a sweet smiling Babe,
　　With St. Joseph she kneels in humility low,
And there offers to Heaven the Father's own Son,
　　Whose wisdom directs all events here below.

Full of wonder and love, holy Simeon draws near;
　　Trembling words float like incense on soft summer air,
As he clasps to his bosom the true Son of God,
　　And returns to the Father a most fervent pray'r.

His eye now beholdeth all Israel's hope
　　And the offering for man, yea, the sole worthy one ;
The great Ruler of Nations rejects not the gift
　　Which the Virginal Mother presents as her son.

In a temple of God far away from our shore
　　The same off'ring was made, although differed the way,
When Most Reverend Archbishop, whose name we revere,
　　Performed Mary's duty that thrice-blessed day.

Fifty years have elapsed since thy form was first robed
  With the garb sacerdotal the Church doth bestow,
And with power of Apostles she thee did invest —
  Greatest power e'er attained by poor mortals below.

The Red Man so savage, the forest's sole lord,
  Sped o'er the blue waves in his birch-bark canoe,
When across the broad breast of the foam-crested main,
  Thou didst bring to him principles holy and true.

On the carpeted meadows, green woodlands, and vales,
  Where now points to the skies our Cathedral's grand spire,
There the Indian Braves with their followers dwelt,
  And their war-dance performed round their bright council fire.

But the hand of the Saviour, through many a strife,
  Led thee on, and all obstacles moved from thy way,
And the waves of Lake Michigan sparkled with joy,
  When first dawned in Milwaukee thy entering day.

The bright spring-time had come, and all nature was glad,
  While enhancing the beauty of mountains and glen ;
In the Church was a season far grander than this,
  'Twas the month of St. Joseph, the meekest of men.

With his feast came the crosier and mitre for thee,
  Blest ensigns of power we all hold so dear,
For they made thee our Bishop, our Shepherd and Guide,
  When God sent thee kindly to dwell with us here.

And beneath thy direction, so prudent and mild,
  Rose temples of God, and our dear lady's shrine,
Where deep tones of the organ in fullness resound,
  And the cloud-piercing prayer with music combines.

Then were schools, too, established and science' broad road
  Was opened to all who its course would pursue,
In its dim-lettered volumes with pleasure to learn,
  Of its wonderful triumphs by principles true.

The pure seraphs above, in life's closely-sealed book,
  Have recorded thy deeds in bright letters of gold ;
And how happy the thought, although time doth conceal,
  At eternity's dawn will its pages unfold !

Eighteen hundred and seventy-five, in its course,
  O'er the waves of the ocean brought honors to thee ;
From the Chair of St. Peter the Pallium was sent
  That has made of Milwaukee an Archbishop's see.

Many years hast thou labored with untiring zeal,
  Ever striving thy children on paths to retain,
Where the flowers of knowledge in loveliness bloom,
  And diffuse rarest perfume o'er valley and plain.

Eighteen hundred and fifty, when our loved Convent School
  Was beginning its course on the hill to pursue,
Never failed thy kind aid, never wearied thy hand,
  'Till our dear Alma Mater stood open to view.

And from all our Cream City's Parochial schools,
  Many children are studying within the loved walls
Of St. Mary's, where, gathering the rich fruits of lore,
  Their school days they finish in these classic halls.

Even those who profess not the faith which we prize,
  Must acknowledge advantages gained by its sway;
And although they embrace not the creed we hold dear,
  Yet they ever must reverence its bright cheering ray.

Then accept, Reverend Prelate, our most cordial thanks
For the kindness bestowed us so many a year;
While exists but a stone of our Convent school walls,
Thy name shall be cherished, thy memory held dear.

From the high court of Heaven may God's choicest gifts
Descend with the blessings of sweet peace and love;
May the pure, snowy wings of the angels surround,
O'er thy silvery locks ever hover the Dove.

May the hand of the Father, who reigneth on high,
Yet preserve thee for years, us thy children to guide;
To strengthen our souls 'gainst the snares of the fiend,
And teach them not follow sin's treacherous tide.

When at last, the dark days of thy pilgrimage o'er,
And afar is seen gleaming the City of Gold,
May its portals of jasper be opened to thee,
Our Most Reverend Archbishop, with all of thy fold.

Oh! when thou shalt enter that home of the blest,
Where angels will bring thy bright crown unto thee,
At the banquet thou 'lt sit with the Saviour of men,
And forever rejoice in — One Grand Jubilee!

ELLA POLLARD.

Harmonische Klänge aus der Ferne.

———

Euer Erzbischöfliche Gnaden!
Hochwürdigſter, hochzuverehrendſter Oberhirte!
Unſer erſter Biſchof und Erzbiſchof!
Hochgefeierter Prieſter Jubilarius!

So weit die Kunde Deiner Jubelfeier ſich verbreitet
Ertönt der Freudenruf: Heil Erzbiſchof! Prieſter=Jubilar!
An MILWAUKEE'S Kindergratulanten wir uns reihen.

Bringen durch Schutzengel Hände unſre Wünſche dar,
Im Vereine mit unſern Lehrerinnen
Den Schulſchweſtern de NOTRE DAME
Zollen wir auch unſre Huldigungen
In der Schweſtern, Schüler Nam'!

Engel an zweihundertfünfzig
Kommen von CALVARIA her,
Von den Deinen, die Dich ehren,
Die Dich lieben, o ſo ſehr.

Gnade woll' der Himmel ſpenden!
Wünſcht KENOSHA'S treue Schaar;
Dort dreihundert Kinder flehen
Für Dein Wohlſein immerdar.

Elm Grove's Schüler wünschen Frieden,
Den das Christkind selbst gebracht,
Hundert Stimmen sich vereinen
In den Sang der heil'gen Nacht.

Aus Sheboygan nah zweihundert
Rufen : Heil ! Erzbischof Heil !
Wir an Deinem Jubelfeste
Nehmen innigsten Antheil.

Auch von Burlington her bringet
Ein zweihundertstimm'ger Chor :
Wolle Gott Eu'r Gnaden schützen !
Schallt's zum Himmel hoch empor.

Beaver Dam schickt Glückeswünsche
An zweihundertfünfzig heut,
Dem geliebten Oberhirten,
Als Tribut der Dankbarkeit.

Madison hat schön gewunden
Einen mystischen Blumenkranz
Aus dreihundert Kinderherzen,
Zu erhöh'n des Festes Glanz.

Gar bescheiden schicket Brighton
Angebind : Vergißmeinnicht ;
Neunzig Sternlein wollen deuten :
Treu der Kirche ! Treu der Pflicht !

Fromm Sanct Kilian hat erflehet ;
Segen zu dem Jubelfest ;
Hundertdreißig Kinder beten :
Segen für des Lebens Rest !

WATERFORD auch gratulirend
Achtzig Wünschlein bringet dar :
Heiterkeit, Gesundheit, Freude,
Und noch viele, viele Jahr!

Von PORT WASHINGTON herunter :
Jubilate! Höchster Hirt!
Wohl dreihundert Kinder singen :
Ehre Ihm, dem Ehr' gebührt!

FRANKLIN mit den lieben Kleinen
Hundertfünfundzwanzig gar :
Hoch Milwaukee's erstem Bischof!
Hent der Priester-Jubilar!

Nun der Schutzgeist SAUKVILLE'S kommet
Leget auf den Festaltar
Noch zweihundert Wünsche innig
Bringet Dir Verehrung dar.

JEFFERSON mit Knaben, Mädchen
Hundertfünfzig gratulirt :
Heil zur gold'nen Jubelfeier!
Vivat unser Oberhirt!

Daß Maria wolle schützen
Euer Gnaden lang noch hier :
Wünscht mit hundert Grüßen WHEATLAND ;
Wird es wünschen für und für.

Auch SAINT FRANCIS STATION sandte
Sechzigfältig Dankgebühr :
Gott belohn' Dein edles Wirken,
Du Wisconsin's schönste Zier!

WAUKESHA entrichtet Wünsche
Ebenso der Liebe Zoll,
Heut an Deinem Ehrentage
Hundertachtzig für Dein Wohl.

WATERTOWN nennt Deinen Namen
Mit Verehrung, Dankbarkeit,
Und als Unterpfand der Liebe
Dir zweihundert Herzen weiht.

OSHKOSH' Engel bringt Verstärkung
Durch zweihundert Stimmen Zahl :
Segne Gott den Oberhirten
Wünschen treue Schäflein all'.

Und WEST BEND mit fünfundsieb'nzig,
Soll's wohl Vorbedeutung sein?
Wünscht des Tag's Diamanten Feier
Jubilar! noch werde Dein.

Aus den Herzen Deiner Schäflein wallen
Diese Wünsche himmelwärts empor ;
O verleih dem Gruß, den Kinder brachten
Huldvoll heute ein geneigtes Ohr!
Deinen Segen uns noch spende
Heut zu dieses Festes Ende.
Nochmals rausch' empor
Jubelnder Festchor!

Heil! Erzbischof! Jubilar! Heil Deinem mühevollen Streben!
Heil dem großen Weinberg! Heil den zarten Reben!

CHANT DES CROATES,   -   -   -   -   *Chatterton*

Catholic Citizen Print